The desire to fit in comes naturally to all of us. As a kid, I discovered the music of my grandpa's generation. Not the coolest thing to listen to in the 80's! I was afraid my friends would think I was weird. Turns out, O'Shae and I have a lot in common. With the love and support of our friends and family, we both learned that our differences don't make us strange, they make us special!

MICHAEL BUBLÉ

BRANDEE BUBLÉ

ILLUSTRATED BY
ELISKA LISKA

O'Shae THE Octopus

SIMPLY READ BOOKS

Down deep beneath the ocean,
In a cozy coral reef,
Lived the neatest little octopus
You'd ever want to meet!

"O'Shae, you're extra special,"
Mom said, time and time again.

"Instead of having eight arms,
You've been blessed, my dear, with ten!"

More arms made it so easy
For O'Shae to lend a hand,
To tidy up his bedroom
Or help Dad sweep piles of sand.

Each afternoon for playtime,
He would swim to Seaweed Park
And swing and climb and seesaw
With his friend Shelton the Shark.

One day some bullies showed up
As the friends began to play—
A lobster nicknamed Lanny
And Mean Mike the Manta Ray.

The bullies cornered Shelton
And said, "Hey you, little shark,
Your friend is just not normal.
Scram! Get out! This is OUR park."

O'Shae felt truly awful.
He had heard what they had said.
"Come on," he sobbed to Shelton.
"Let's go somewhere else instead."

"Cheer up, O'Shae," said Shelton.
"Your two extra arms are great.
You can do way more with ten
Than you can do with only eight."

"You're right!" O'Shae told Shelton,
And he grabbed his friend and twirled.
He spun that shark in circles.
He became a Tilt-a-Whirl!

They didn't need a playground.
He would make himself the rides!
Some arms could be the swing set,
And some arms could be the slides.

O'Shae could bend and straighten.
He could spin and sway and twist.

He became the best park ever—
One that no fish could resist!

Soon there was a lineup
Stretching miles across the sand
To ride O'Shae the Octopus
With the ten amazing hands.

Mean Mike and Lanny Lobster
Came by later on to say,
"We're sorry. Please forgive us.
You're sensational, O'Shae!"

On the last ride of the evening,
On the swings in O'Shae Park,
Swung a laughing manta ray,
A lobster and a shark.

Tiffany & Kallie, thank you for helping me make O'Shae "sensational"!
Bruce & Sarah, this wouldn't be possible without you! Thank you!
—BRANDEE

Published in 2014 by Simply Read Books www.simplyreadbooks.com
Text © 2014 Brandee Bublé Illustrations © 2014 Eliska Liska

Library and Archives Canada Cataloguing in Publication

Bublé, Brandee, author

O'Shea the octopus / written by Brandee Bublé ; illustrated by Eliska Liska.

ISBN 978-1-927018-56-9 (bound)

I. Liska, Eliska, 1981–, illustrator II. Title.

PS8603.U275O85 2014   JC813'.6   C2013-907305-1

We gratefully acknowledge for their financial support of our publishing program
the Canada Council for the Arts, the BC Arts Council, and the Government of
Canada through the Canada Book Fund (CBF).

Manufactured in Malaysia
Book design by Naomi MacDougall

10 9 8 7 6 5 4 3 2 1

To O'Shae. You amaze me every day with your enormous heart
and brilliant mind! You make me prouder than you can imagine.
You mean more to me than you'll ever know. I love you.

BRANDEE

To my three extra special beings: Dana, Lola and Nino.

ELISKA

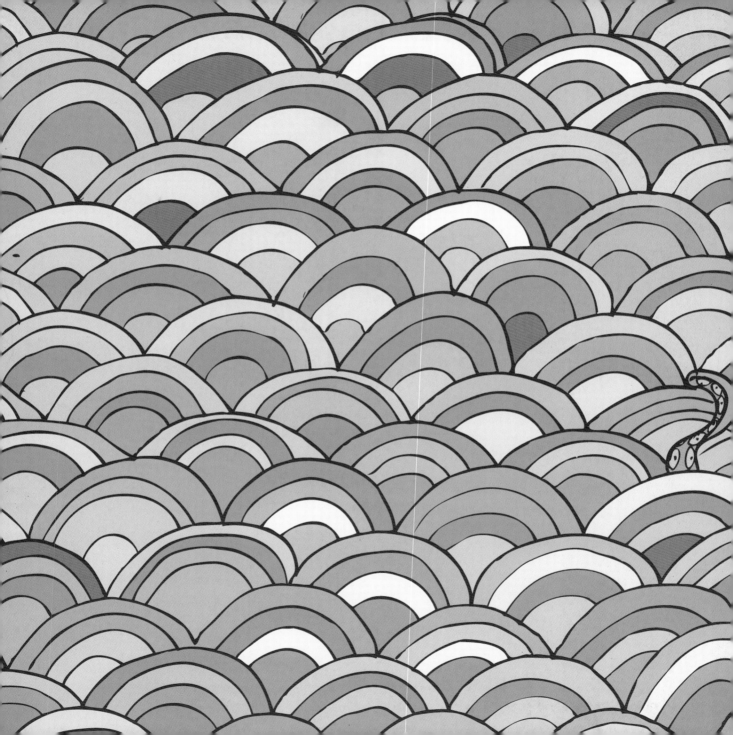